Follow your dreams
Katerina Bernius

www.mascotbooks.com

The Magical Flower

©2020 Katerina Bernius. All Rights Reserved. No part of this publication may be reproduced, stored in a retrieval system or transmitted in any form by any means electronic, mechanical, or photocopying, recording or otherwise without the permission of the author.

For more information, please contact:
Mascot Books
620 Herndon Parkway, Suite 320
Herndon, VA 20170
info@mascotbooks.com

Library of Congress Control Number: 2020902839

CPSIA Code: PRT0620A
ISBN-13: 978-1-64307-529-7

Printed in the United States

It was a hot day in North Massapequa, and friends Katerina, Keira, and Erin were planting a garden. **Suddenly, one seed started to glow!**

"*It's a magical flower!*" Erin yelled. All three girls ran inside the house.

Katerina, Keira, and Erin had a snack and watched the magical flower grow from the window.

"What do you think it will do?" Katerina asked.

"I don't know," Keira said.

When the magical flower had grown all the way, Katerina decided the only way to learn more about the flower was to go outside again.

Slowly, she walked up to it.
Suddenly, the flower started talking!

Katerina ran back to Keira and Erin. "Are you okay?" they asked.

"I'm fine," Katerina said. **"It's a talking flower!"**

Together, the girls walked up to the flower again. "Hi, girls," the flower said.

"Do you think the magical flower is nice?" Katerina whispered to Keira and Erin.

"Of course the magical flower is nice," Erin said.

Katerina was a little scared, but she took a deep breath and said, *"Hi."*

Suddenly, the flower started to glow again. Then, it came out of the dirt!

The girls were very surprised. Then the flower asked, "Do you want to play ring around the rosie with me?"

The girls agreed, and they all played ring around the rosie.

Then, two seeds dropped from the magical flower, and two more magical flowers grew from them.

Now Keira and Erin had flower friends, too! Katerina, Keira, and Erin had so much fun with their new magical flower friends.

The next day when the girls came outside to play, all the magical flowers were droopy.

"What's wrong?" Katerina asked her flower.

"We are droopy because it's almost winter," her flower said. "But it's okay. *We will be back next year.*"

Winter came, and it was cold and snowy. Katerina, Keira, and Erin missed their magical flower friends.

"Do you think they'll be back in the spring?" Keira asked.

"I hope so," Katerina said.

One day in the spring, Katerina, Keira, and Erin went outside to play and saw something glowing in the garden again. **Their magical flowers had returned!**

"Do you want to play?" the magical flowers asked.

"**Yes!**" they said, and they were happy all day long.

About the Author

Katerina T. Bernius is only nine years old, and she lives in North Massapequa, New York with her mom, dad, younger sister, Annabel, and her pet snake, Cupcake. Katerina's favorite subjects are reading and writing. She started writing books in 3rd grade because she loved reading and writing so much. She also enjoys dancing, competitive dancing, Tae Kwon Do, and spending time with her kooky family. Katerina wants to encourage people to follow their dreams and to, "do something if you think you can."